Krish

Lucas T-C

Kayleigh

Jake

Arun

Sophie

Thank you to Wembrook
Primary School, Nuneaton,
for helping with the endpapers.

For Casey, Sean,
and Eamon—V.T.

To Henry-James Christie
with love—K.P.

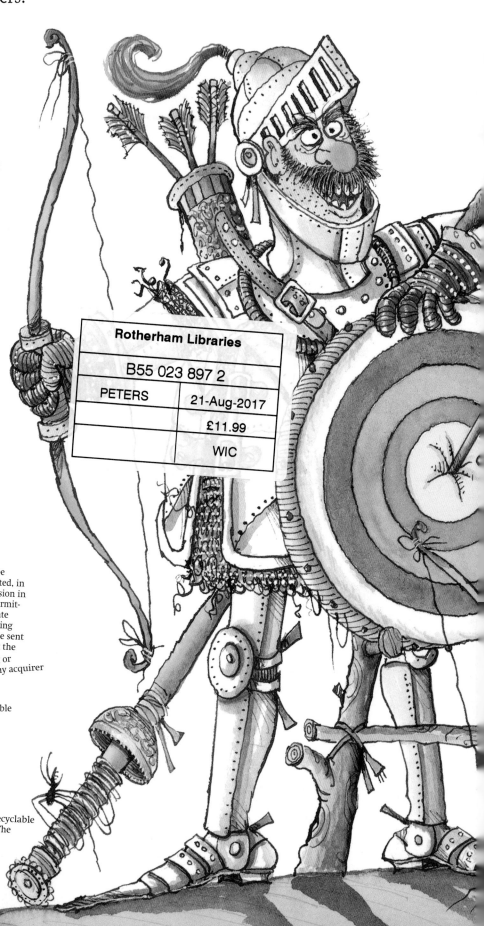

OXFORD
UNIVERSITY PRESS

Great Clarendon Street, Oxford OX2 6DP

Oxford University Press is a department of the
University of Oxford. It furthers the University's
objective of excellence in research, scholarship,
and education by publishing worldwide.
Oxford is a registered trade mark of
Oxford University Press in the UK and
n certain other countries

Database right Oxford University Press (maker)

First published in 2017

British Library Cataloguing in Publication Data available

ISBN: 978-0-19-275947-4 (hardback)

10 9 8 7 6 5 4 3 2 1

Printed in China

Paper used in the production of this book is a natural, recyclable
product made from wood grown in sustainable forests. The
manufacturing process conforms to the environmental
regulations of the country of origin

www.winnieandwilbur.com

VALERIE THOMAS AND KORKY PAUL

Winnie and Wilbur

THE NAUGHTY KNIGHT

OXFORD

UNIVERSITY PRESS

One day, when Winnie the Witch
and her big black cat Wilbur
were flying high over the mountains,
Winnie looked down and saw
an enormous castle.

'Look at that beautiful castle, Wilbur,' Winnie said.
'Let's go and have a look.'

But when they swooped down to the castle
they found it was just a ruin.
'Blithering broomsticks,' said Winnie.
'We are hundreds of years too late.'

Then Winnie had a wonderful idea.
She waved her magic wand, shouted,

'Abracadabra!'

. . . and there was a beautiful castle, just the way it used to be, full of people just the way they used to be.

CRASH! CLANK! CLUNK!

The drawbridge was being lowered over the moat for the king and queen! After them came flags, lovely ladies, and knights in shining armour.

Winnie and Wilbur landed high up in a tower.

'Oooh!' said Winnie. 'Today must
be a special tournament.
We'll go and see what happens.
But first we have to look right.'

Winnie waved her magic wand, shouted,

'Abracadabra!'

and there she was, looking just like the other lovely ladies. Well, she looked a bit like the other lovely ladies.

And Wilbur was a tiny knight in shining armour.

Winnie hid her broomstick, tucked her wand up her sleeve, just in case, and they hurried off to watch the tournament.

The first contest was archery.
There were some very good archers,
but the best was Sir Roderick.
Sir Roderick was huge. He had a big
red face and a big loud voice.

His three arrows all hit the bullseye.
'I am the winner,' he shouted.
'I am the best archer in the kingdom!'

'There is one more archer,' said Winnie.
'Sir Wilbur is an amazing archer.'
'Ha ha ha,' laughed everybody when they
saw Sir Wilbur.
'Ha ha ha ha,' laughed Sir Roderick.

'Abracadabra!'

whispered Winnie,
and she waved her arm.

Sir Wilbur shot the first arrow into the bullseye.

The second arrow split the first arrow.

The third arrow split the second one.

Amazing! Incredible! Unbelievable!
Sir Wilbur was the winner.

'Grrrr,' snarled Sir Roderick.

BIFF!

'Now for the jousting,' said the king.
Sir Roderick leapt onto an enormous black horse.

Sir Roderick knocked the first knight off his horse.

Sir Wilbur.

BANG!

Then the second, the third, the fourth, until only one knight was left.

Winnie lifted Sir Wilbur onto an enormous white horse.
'Hold on tight, Wilbur,' she whispered.
'Remember my wand is up my sleeve.'

Into the lists rode Sir Wilbur and Sir Roderick.
They galloped towards each other.
Winnie waved her arm.
'Abracadabra!'

BIFF!

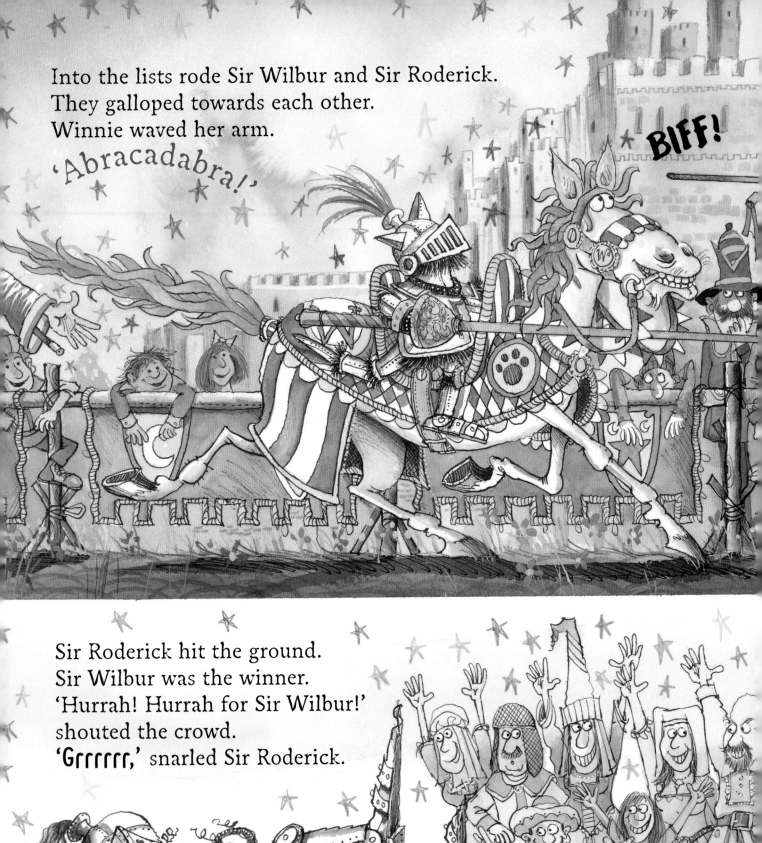

Sir Roderick hit the ground.
Sir Wilbur was the winner.
'Hurrah! Hurrah for Sir Wilbur!'
shouted the crowd.
'Grrrrrr,' snarled Sir Roderick.

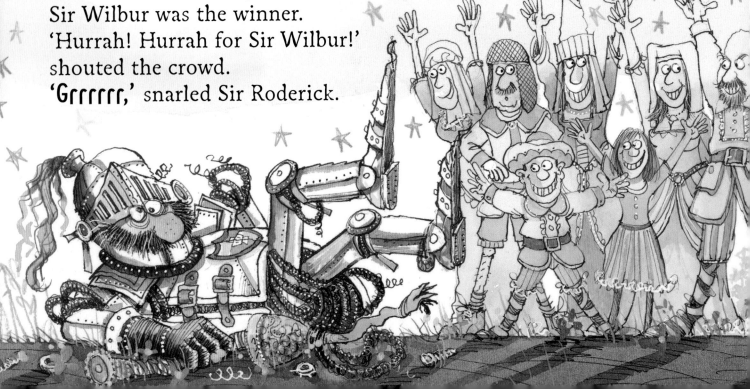

BANG!

'It's time for the banquet,' said the king.
'Sir Wilbur will sit next to me.'
'GGGRRRRRR!' snarled Sir Roderick.
He was furious.

He rushed into the Great Hall,
tipped over the soup,
smashed all the pies, and
jumped in the jellies.

What a mess!

She waved her magic sleeve,
whispered,

'Abracadabra!'

and Sir Roderick started to shrink.
He got smaller and smaller . . .

'Hmmm,' said Winnie. 'Sir Roderick needs to be taught a lesson.'

until he was the same size as Sir Wilbur. 'Grrrrrr,' said Sir Roderick.

'Now for the banquet,' Winnie said. She waved her magic sleeve, whispered,

'Abracadabra!'

. . . and there was a magnificent
banquet, even better than the first.

'There is some mighty
magic here today,' said the king.

'Take off your visor, Sir Wilbur.
We want to see your face.'

Oh no!! The king would not be pleased
to see that Sir Wilbur was a cat!

Winnie snatched up Wilbur, raced up the stairs, jumped onto her broomstick, and zoomed up into the sky.

They were soon home again.

'Castles are exciting,' said Winnie.
'But it's lovely to be home again,
isn't it, Wilbur?'

'Purr, purr, purr,' said Wilbur.

Jacob

Micha

Ethan

Amber

Poppy

Sofia

Erin